D1038267

NORTHAMPTON COMMUNITY
DISCARDED
COLLEGE LIBRARY

NORTHAMPTON COUNTY AREA
Learning Resources Center
Bethlehem, Pa. 18017
COMMUNITY COLLEGE

THE POOR FIDDLER

A folk festival in Vienna

FRANZ GRILLPARZER

THE POOR FIDDLER

Translated from the German by
Alexander and Elizabeth Henderson

Introduction by Ivar Ivask

Illustrations by Lilly Kehlmann

FREDERICK UNGAR PUBLISHING CO.
NEW YORK

Frontispiece illustration
from the picture archives of the
Österreichische Nationalbibliothek,
Fonds Albertina

Printed in the United States of America

Library of Congress Catalog Card No. 66-19471

INTRODUCTION

> ". . . For it is by perfection of form that poetry enters life, external life. True emotion can convey only what lies within. But it is the task of all art to exemplify the inner life by the outer surface." [1]

The Poor Fiddler, the story of a failure, is told with genuine sympathy and yet objective detachment. It could well have had as its author one of the great Russian novelists of the last century—Gogol, Dostoevsky, or Turgenev. The first-person narrator characterizes himself as a dramatist and a passionate lover of his fellow men, especially the common people. He also stresses his strong anthropological bent and psychological curiosity. Indeed, he believes that "In truth, no one can understand the lives of the famous unless he has entered into the feelings of the humble. An invisible but continuous thread connects the brawling of drunken market porters with the

[1] "*. . . Denn die vollendete Form ist es, wodurch die Poesie ins Leben tritt, ins* äußere *Leben. Die Wahrheit der Empfindung gibt nur das Innere; es ist aber Aufgabe aller Kunst, ein* Inneres *durch ein* Außeres *darzustellen.*"—Franz Grillparzer, *Sämtliche Werke,* eds. Peter Frank and Karl Pörnbacher (Munich, 1964), III, 286

strife of the sons of gods, and Juliet, Dido or Medea exist in embryo within every young servant girl. . . ." This rather astonishing credo of realism comes from a writer who was a contemporary of Goethe, writing at the height of idealism and romanticism in literature. The story was begun in 1831, completed some ten years later, but not published until 1847.

The author, Franz Grillparzer (1791–1872), was born and died in Vienna. His father was a lawyer; his mother possessed great musical talent. Grillparzer studied law at the University of Vienna and was later employed as a civil servant in various positions, finally as director of the State Archives (1832–56). After his mother's suicide in a fit of religious madness, he set out on an Italian journey. A poem, *"Die Ruinen von Campo Vaccino"* [The Ruins of Campo Vaccino],* written on this journey, was received with hostility in court circles. In this poem, Grillparzer expressed sympathy with the fact that ancient Rome had had to yield to Christianity. Because of this, he was suspected of anticlerical sentiments by the ever-suspicious secret police of Metternich's reactionary regime.

* When works have not appeared in English, literal translations are given in brackets; titles of published English translations are given within parentheses.

From that time on, he was beset by difficulties with the censors. In 1821, Grillparzer met Katharina Fröhlich, and a lifelong relationship outside marriage ensued. He traveled in Germany (1826 and 1847), France (1836), and visited Constantinople and Athens (1843). He knew personally many of his great contemporaries such as Goethe, Beethoven, Heine, and Hebbel. When his comedy *Weh dem, der lügt* [Woe to Him Who Lies], written in 1838, failed at its première, Grillparzer decided to publish no more plays. In 1856, he was retired with the rank of Court Councillor (*Hofrat*) and in 1861 was made a member of the *Herrenhaus* (House of Lords). Yet these honors came far too late to assuage Grillparzer's bitter awareness that he was not really at home in his own country: a very Austrian fate.

Grillparzer is considered by most critics to be the greatest Austrian dramatist. This claim is based on his verse plays, in which he tried to fuse elements of the Spanish and Austrian baroque and the Viennese popular theater with the classical drama of Goethe and Schiller. Grillparzer's deepest artistic sympathies were certainly with the colorful and passionate Spanish baroque dramatists, Calderón, Lope de Vega, and Tirso da Molina (many of whose plays he minutely annotated in his diaries); yet his critical mind was almost equally attracted by the rationalism of Enlightenment, which in Austria took the form of "Josephinism." Grillparzer's dramatic figures are often caught in the tragic dilemma of being compelled to act but hesitating to do so, because all action of necessity results in some guilt. His plays on Greek themes, such as *Sappho* (1819), or *Das goldene Vließ* [The Golden Fleece] (1822), are less successful than those that deal with Austrian and Slav history—for example, *Ein Bruderzwist in Habsburg* [Family Strife in Hapsburg] (1873), perhaps his greatest dramatic achievement. The love story of Hero and Leander has found a poetically sensitive presentation in the play *Des Meeres und der Liebe Wellen* [The Waves of the Sea and of Love] (1831); it reveals the dramatist's Austrian gift for creating psychologically believable, strong women characters. The English critic Ronald Peacock comments perceptively on Grillparzer's dramatic art: "In poetic power, in the creative use of language, he is inferior to the lyric poets of the great periods—Novalis, Hölderlin, George, Rilke; inferior even to a prose rhapsodist like Herder. *But in his sense of reality he is unique,* if we except the rather special case of Goethe. It may be that his Austrian nationality has something to do with it; for Austria, as the centre of power of the Holy Roman Empire and later the Austro-Hungarian, came nearer to political success than the modern German Reich has ever done." [2] This unique sense of reality stood Grillparzer in good stead when he wrote *The Poor Fiddler.*

Looking for parallels in German literature, we find a similar early rebellion against the canons of idealism and romanticism in Georg Büchner's story *Lenz* (written around 1835). "I demand of art," we read, "that it be life and the possibility that it might exist—nothing else matters; we then have no need to ask whether it is beautiful or ugly. The sense that what has been created has life stands above the other two precepts and is the only criterion in art. . . . Idealism is the most humiliating of insults to human nature. Let them try just once to immerse themselves in the life of the humble people and then

[2] Ronald Peacock, *The Poet in the Theatre* (New York, 1960), p. 62 [my ital.—I.I]. For the reception of Grillparzer's drama in the English-speaking world, see Arthur Burkhard, *Franz Grillparzer in England and America* (Vienna, 1961).

reproduce this again in all its movements, its implications, in its subtle, scarcely discernible play of expression. . . ." [3]

Georg Büchner seemed to have the makings of a German Dostoevsky, but he died prematurely in 1837 at the age of twenty-four, and was duly discovered only much later by the naturalists and expressionists. So-called German "poetic realism," which dominated German literature from about Büchner's death until the final decades of the past century, had little of his bite and sheer creative energy, even less of his profound social concern. Büchner remained a lonely pioneer without establishing a German "great tradition" of the realistic novel that might be placed alongside the classics of the Russian, French, and English writers of the age. The German novel and novella of the later nineteenth century basically owed more to idealism and a lingering romanticism than to realism in the sense given it by the great European novelists.

Dostoevsky is supposed to have remarked once that "We all came out of Gogol's *Overcoat*." The same could be said in relation to the Aus-

[3] Georg Büchner, *Complete Plays and Prose,* trans. Carl Richard Mueller (New York, 1963), p. 151

trian novelists after Grillparzer's truly seminal story *The Poor Fiddler*. More often than not the protagonists of Austrian stories have been variations on the theme first played by the poor fiddler on his cracked violin. A veritable procession of complex-ridden, indecisive anti-heroes, "superfluous men" (well-known to readers of the Russian novel), failures in practical life but pure of heart, people the Austrian novel and stage to this very day. They are usually presented with warm understanding and a psychological insight such that even those works conceived well before Freud may strike one as being positively "Freudian." To name just a few random examples of this Austrian "great tradition": the misunderstood, miserly country parson in Adalbert Stifter's story, *Kalkstein* [Limestone], the first version of which was written in 1848, perhaps in competition with Grillparzer's story (which was hailed by Stifter as a masterpiece); Marie von Ebner-Eschenbach's *Dorf- und Schloßgeschichten* [Village and Castle Stories] (1883) contains a whole gallery of related types; Ferdinand von Saar's subtle analysis of the make-believe world of *Lieutenant Burda* (1889); Arthur Schnitzler's *Lieutenant Gustl* (1900) and his early, effective use of interior monologue to render the inner turmoil of an average fellow caught in an insoluble dilemma that involves his honor or dishonor, life or death; Robert Musil's first novel, *Die Verwirrungen des Zöglings Törless* (Young Törless) (1906), about the psychological and physiological confusions of adolescence; Rilke's hypersensitive poet, Malte, the subject of *Die Aufzeichnungen des Malte Laurids Brigge* (The Notebooks of Malte Laurids Brigge), in Paris, and Albert Ehrenstein's helpless *Tubutsch* in Vienna (both published in 1910) ; the host of frustrated and guilt-ridden bachelors in Kafka's stories and novels; Musil's paradoxical *Der Mann ohne Eigenschaften* (The Man without Qualities) (1931–33); the pathetic Lieutenant Trotta in Joseph Roth's novel, *Radetzkymarsch* (1932) ; Heimito von Doderer's widowed civil servant turned voyeur, Julius Zihal, in *Die erleuchteten Fenster* [The Illuminated Windows], and his Lieutenant Melzer whose separation from reality is gradually overcome in *Die Strudlhofstiege* [The Strudlhof Stairs], both published in 1951; and, in conclusion, Herbert Eisenreich's long story, *Der Urgroßvater* [The Great-grandfather] (1964) , in which the rather ordinary protagonist becomes so preoccupied with his origins that he loses touch with reality. More than a century of a fascinatingly and closely interrelated narrative tradition! [4]

Obviously the Austrian Franz Grillparzer has been more fortunate than his German contemporary Georg Büchner. *The Poor Fiddler* did become the fountainhead of a rich prose tradition in which the "Insulted and Injured" (to use an apt formula by Dostoevsky), the surprising transformations of the poor fiddler, Jacob, have reappeared again and again. There are many reasons for this occurring in Austrian and not in German literature. The scope of this introduction permits to list only a few, and even these merely in passing. First of all, the Austrians are conservative *par excellence* and therefore great supporters of tradition (to the frequent grief of Austrian innovators and revolutionaries); secondly, Protestant ideal-

[4] The Austrian theater is no exception to this psychological curiosity: in his play, *Der Alpenkönig und der Menschenfeind* [The King of the Alps and the Misanthrope] (1828), Ferdinand Raimund created one of the first presentations of a split personality in world literature; Johann Nestroy entitled a play, *Der Zerrissene* (A Man Full of Nothing) (1844); Hugo von Hofmannsthal's most famous comedy is called *Der Schwierige* [The Difficult Man] (1921), about a man who is afraid to act and so terribly complicated that in the end the marriage proposal has to be made by the bride-to-be herself. These are but three examples; many more could be cited.

ism never had great appeal in Catholic Austria; and, thirdly, the baroque world view and style, oddly surviving well into the nineteenth century and beyond, immunized the Austrian writers against the lure of German romanticism. It could be formulated—boldly and paradoxically—that Austrian literature has been attracted time and time again to a kind of baroque realism, characterized by a constant tension between illusion and reality, being and doing. It is an existential tension that is to be borne, if not in faith, then at least with stoical equanimity, and it does *not* annihilate reality itself. After all, the Roman emperor and stoic philosopher Marcus Aurelius died in Vienna and it was on Austrian soil that he wrote the following remarks: "In the life of a man, his time is but a moment, his being an incessant flux, his senses a dim rushlight, his body a prey of worms, his soul an unquiet eddy, his fortune dark, and his fame doubtful. In short, all that is body is as coursing waters, all that is of the soul as dreams and vapors. . . ." [5] The emperor is still fondly remembered by the Viennese. Heimito von Doderer claimed only recently that it is "Marcus Aurelius Antoninus,

[5] Marcus Aurelius, *Meditations,* trans. Maxwell Staniforth (Baltimore, 1964), p. 51.

with whose modern as well as profound notes Viennese literary history begins a few years before A.D. 180."[6] Indeed, the proverbial gaiety of the Viennese is not a diagnosis but a therapy for a fundamentally melancholy, self-analytical people at the crossroads of several nations (to refer to an enlightening formula by Hans Weigel). Austrian literature is by and large more deeply embedded in the country's landscape, filled with more affection for its capital and its society, evokes more lovingly a whole "way of life" than we are accustomed to in the literature of Germany. There is no doubt that Grillparzer is a truly representative son of his people.

Grillparzer was oversensitive, moody, hypochondriac, easily depressed, irritable, melancholy, self-tormenting; in short, an extremely complex man. (When traveling, he wanted nothing so much as to be home again; back in Vienna, however, he felt stifled and longed for freedom abroad.) His autobiography, abundant literary criticism, and dramatic works bear witness to this complexity. Yet nowhere does he present himself with as much clairvoyance and mature detachment

[6] Heimito von Doderer, "Einleitung," in Toni Schneider's *Österreich* (Zürich, 1958), p. 22.

as in his story about the poor fiddler. It seems truly to be an objective correlative of his own life and doubts, a self-contained work of art in no need of supporting biographical explanation to be fully appreciated and understood. Nevertheless, it constitutes an additional attraction for anyone acquainted with Grillparzer's biography to observe how the author's own taciturnity and his stiffly correct behavior (occasionally animated by plain human curiosity) are so well reflected in the outline portrait of the first-person narrator of the story. Although the fate of the poor fiddler occupies undisputedly the center of the stage, the story certainly gains in poignancy from the constant subtle counterpoint with the narrator's character and the framework that it adds to the story of the very much more unhappy and confused man—the fiddler.

But the attentive reader may be left wondering in the end whether Jacob has not lived more intensely and deeply amidst all his tribulations than the narrator ever has or will. Thus Grillparzer challenges through his art our very concept of what constitutes meaningful reality and healthy normalcy. We may ask further if Grillparzer is not only reflected in the courteous first-person narrator of the tale but, perhaps, in Jacob as well. Does not Jacob's highly questionable "art" mirror some of the Austrian dramatist's own self-lacerating doubts concerning the ultimate quality of his art when compared with the celebrated achievements of Goethe and Schiller? In Jacob, we find Grillparzer's own love of music, sense of measure, love of truth, enthusiasm, and penchant for pedantry, developed by the drudgery of office work that left only the evenings for creative activity. But then the effort of Jacob's life and art is consummated on an altogether different plane from that of the author, namely that of self-sacrifice and religious meaning. Jacob dies from the aftereffects of having braved the cold waters of the Danube to save some children from the floods. The fact that the enlightened rationalist, Grillparzer, tries to mask his embarrassment at this religious turn of events in his own story—by making Jacob brave the floodwaters yet another time, merely to salvage the tax books of a gardener—in no way devalues the tears that the woman, whom Jacob never was able to win, sheds for him. In the end, his cracked violin shares pride of place on her living-room wall with the crucifix. Grillparzer intimates here a solution for poor Jacob that was no longer open to himself. Thus Jacob, too, *is* and is *not* the author. The perplexing tension and mystery of great art remain intact.

It was around 1847–48 or a little later that Grillparzer replied to a question as to how he had found the real-life inspiration for his story:

> Quite by accident! For many years, I had been taking my meals at the restaurant "Zum Jägerhorn" in the Spiegelgasse. Often a poor fiddler came there to play. He attracted attention by the remarkable cleanliness of his shabby clothing, and his clumsy movements were touchingly comical. This old man always expressed gratitude for a gift with a short Latin phrase, which indicated an education and better days in the past. Suddenly he stopped coming and stayed away for a long time. Then the great flood of 1830 came. The Brigittenau, where a popular Saint's day is celebrated each year with a folk festival and much merrymaking, was striken hardest of all. I knew that the poor fiddler lived there, and as he did not come to play any more, I assumed that he had died as one of the many flood victims. I was asked to write a story for a pocket-almanac, and so I attempted one in

which my poor good friend plays the main part.[7]

So simple and humble was the initial germ of our story. The final work was the result of more than ten years of writing and rewriting. In the story—now for the first time in an English translation that does it full justice—Grillparzer places against the background of a popular Viennese holiday the encounter between two men, one a somewhat sullen, sober dramatist, the other a naïve but serene beggar who makes a living with his fiddle. Both are very lonely and—in differing degrees—artists. Yet the one is at least sure of his social status and superior education, while the other reveals in his poverty flashes of better days, even a certain nobility in his demeanor. The narrator is fascinated by "people" in general, while the beggar is flattered by the gentleman's attention. What attracts the gentleman's curiosity in the first place, and thus triggers the action of the whole story, is that the seventy-year-old beggar plays the violin, following a score, and concludes the performance with a Latin phrase. The gentleman is struck by the incongruity of the caterwauling music and the surprising presence of a score, the very obvious

[7] Grillparzer, *Sämtliche Werke* (Munich, 1964), III, 1229

distance between intent and realization. This discrepancy turns out to be the main theme of the story. It is repeated later in other symbolic gestures. The old man shares his room with some journeymen, but with chalk draws a line of demarcation to separate his cleaner living area from theirs; when he dares to return the kiss of the woman he loves, he does so through a glass door.

In the case of the poor fiddler, reality is so hostile and unattainable that he has no other escape than into the ideal. One of the most penetrating analyses of the story was written by J. P. Stern:

> The annihilating conclusion towards which this quiet, unadorned story takes us is no less than the intimation of a deep and consistent distrust of the substantial world, which appears as a place radically incapable of yielding form and substance to the good will. The pure heart, in this vision, remains disembodied. The value of every thing in the world, of art even—its "objective value"—is as nothing to the purity and goodness and devotion that resides in the heart, mutely, unexpressed, perhaps inexpressible. The rift between being and doing, the severing of intention from realization, of spirit from mat-

ter—even the all but tangible "matter" of music —is complete.[8]

Reality has been everything but kind to Jacob in a life that seems to have consisted of nothing but a series of defeats or failures, depending on the vantage point of the judging reader. Born into a rich and influential family of a court councillor, with brothers who easily surpassed him in school by "jumping like chamois from peak to peak," Jacob would have been happy as a craftsman. "I would have liked nothing better than to become a turner or a compositor," he admits in awareness of his natural limitations. Yet such a solution would have been a disgrace for his family, and so the father inflicts upon his son one punishment after another, without the son in his meek obedience ever daring to challenge this cruel and unjust authority. Early in his life, Jacob loses his mother. When he learns of the death of his father, he faints from emotion, regretting that he did not have the opportunity to ask for his father's forgiveness. Devotion and submission could hardly be carried to more intolerable lengths. One is reminded of Kafka's stories *The Judgment* and *Metamorphosis*, with their nightmarish themes of in-

[8] J. P. Stern, *Re-interpretations* (London, 1964), p. 74.

feriority complexes before paternal authority. (Heinz Politzer has explored the fascination and repulsion felt by the modern Austrian writer toward Grillparzer's story.) [9]

Jacob's job as a humble copyclerk is selected for him by his father. He is kept under constant surveillance, as if he were an irresponsible child. When Jacob finds sudden solace in a simple song that he hears from the neighboring grocer's daughter, Barbara, and visits her in order to get the score for the song, he is expelled from his parental home. But this song, nevertheless, marks a turning point in the life of Jacob, for he takes up the violin again, which he had forgotten since the days of his first instruction. Others may play Bach or Mozart, but no one plays *"den lieben Gott."* It is this that the poor fiddler strives for in his improvisations every evening, until he is reprimanded by his weary neighbors. And they are absolutely right by all normal standards, because the cacophony seems heavenly only to the musician's own ear and, Grillparzer seems to imply, perhaps to God.

Jacob's hopeless naïveté and clumsiness alienated him from his father and his brothers,

[9] "Die Verwandlung des armen Spielmanns," in *Forum* (Vienna, October 1958), pp. 372–75

later from the other clerks in the office where he is employed, and, finally, makes him lose the grocer's daughter to a butcher (which may remind some readers of the way Kafka's "hunger artist" is replaced by a strapping panther). After his father's death, Jacob is even swindled out of his meager inheritance. He dies from exerting his last strength to save a gardener's tax books and a bit of money. In short, Grillparzer has presented to us the tale of a total failure in practical life. A failure because his proud father could not accept that one of his sons would become a mere craftsman? Is Jacob crushed by an overwhelming father complex—somewhat like Georg Bendemann in Kafka's *The Judgment*? This question certainly cannot and should not be answered unequivocally. Jacob's character is not merely the sum total of his environment. He has had, after all, the remarkable resilience of spirit to turn music into a religious escape, which has helped him to maintain a basic dignity, to achieve a stoic fortitude, and has given him the serenity, even a childlike gaiety, admired by the narrator. Art as a sublimation, a redemption from life's miseries—a familiar theme. Yet Grillparzer's story does not end there, for the "art" of Jacob is that of a deluded amateur, hence art proper cannot be called his salvation. If there is any salvation at all, it is strictly outside reality, a religious act of grace.

After the poor fiddler's tragic death, the narrator visits the butcher's family. He sees Jacob's fiddle on the wall "arranged symmetrically" opposite the crucifix. His idea is to buy the fiddle as a remembrance of the queer old fellow. Grillparzer could have added such a transaction as the last ironic twist to his story. Yet at this point, after the self-sacrifice of Jacob, hard practical reality is touched by the world of the spirit, and Barbara refuses to sell the violin, bursting into tears. What is she weeping about? Simply that the world is as it is, that Jacob deserved better treatment from her, or that his death was unnecessary? The story opens on a note of tumultuous gaiety among the holiday crowd; it ends with the tears of one woman, mutely witnessed by the narrator, "a passionate lover of his fellow men." The reader may ask whether the narrator was changed by the experience or was it merely another anecdote, another psychological "case" for him. And what is *the reader's* judgment and conclusion? Grillparzer's realism is a complex one, a baroque realism in which we still sense the tension between illusion and reality, heaven and hell. Although they are more subdued in the Austria of the nineteenth century, the metaphysical categories are still there, subtly implied by the Austrian writer in the narrative fabric of psychological realism. Grillparzer compares, at the beginning, the holiday crowd to a surging flood: ". . . And at last two rivers flow on triumphantly over and under each other—the Danube Canal follows its old river bed, the more swollen stream of people bursts forth from the narrows of the bridge in an all-submerging flood, to form a wide, turbulent lake." In the end it is the Danube, flooded in actuality, that claims the life of Jacob. It is against this background of billowing anonymous masses and raging forces of nature that Grillparzer has chosen to place the spiritual dignity of an individual fate, however ridiculous and insignificant it may appear in the eyes of the world, like a calm ship bound for other shores.

IVAR IVASK

St. Olaf College
Northfield, Minnesota

THE POOR FIDDLER

In Vienna the Sunday after the July full moon is a genuine people's holiday, if ever there was one. Every year on that day and the day after, the people give themselves a party; they are at once hosts and guests, and any members of the upper classes who put in an appearance can do so only as part of the people. This is no occasion for being standoffish; at least it wasn't as recently as a few years ago.

On this day the people of Brigittenau celebrate the dedication of their own saint's church, and with them those of Augarten, Leopoldstadt and the Prater, all linked together in one unbroken chain of jollification. St. Bridget's fair marks happy days for the working folk and they look forward to it from one year to the next. Long awaited, this Saturnalian revel comes round at last. A great uproar then takes possession of the quiet, easygoing town. A swell of people fills the streets, with a clatter of footsteps and a rumble of talk pierced now and then by a cry or shout. Distinctions of calling vanish: citizen and soldier alike are borne on by the tide. At the city gates the push gathers force. The way out is captured, lost, then recaptured, and finally conquered. But next the Danube bridge presents a new obstacle. Another victory, and at last two rivers flow on triumphantly over and under each other—the Danube Canal follows its old river bed, the more swollen stream of people bursts forth from the narrows of the bridge in an all-submerging flood, to form a wide, turbulent lake. A stranger might find the portents dangerous. But the uproar is one of joy, of pleasure unconfined.

Between the city and the bridge hackney-cabriolets are drawn up waiting for the real hierophants of these celebrations—the children of labor and service. Overloaded as they are, the cabs fly through the throng at a gallop, and the crowd divides just in time and closes up again at once, unafraid and unharmed. For in Vienna there is an unwritten pact between vehicle and man, an agreement not to run anyone over, however fast the pace, and not to be run over, however inattentive one may be.

Every second the interval between one cab and the next gets smaller. Smart, upper-class turnouts begin to join the procession, which comes to a halt again and again. The cabs don't fly any more. At last, five or six hours before nightfall, the individual molecules of horses and carriages are compressed into one solid row of traffic, which obstructs itself and is further obstructed by arrivals from all the side streets, and makes nonsense of the old proverb that it is better to be poorly driven than to walk. The ladies in their finery sit in the seemingly motionless vehicles, stared at, pitied, made fun of. Unused to the everlasting waiting, a Holstein black suddenly rears up, as though it wanted to make its way out over the top of the cab blocking its way in front—which is obviously what the screaming women and children populating the plebeian vehicle seem to fear. The darting *fiaker,* for once untrue to his nature, angrily tots up his loss in having to take three hours on a journey he normally whisks through in five minutes. The drivers quarrel, shout, exchange insults, with every now and then a lash of the whip.

At length, since it's in the nature of things for the most obstinate standstill to be an unperceived advance all the same, a ray of hope appears even in this *status quo.* The first trees of the Augarten and Brigittenau come into view. Land! Land in sight! Land ahoy! All troubles are forgotten. Those who have come by carriage get out and join the crowd on foot. Sounds of distant dance music float across and are greeted with cheers by the newcomers. And so on and onward until the wide harbor opens ahead, the harbor of pleasure where woods and meadows, music and dancing, wine and victuals, galanty shows and tightrope walkers, lights and fireworks all come together in one Land of Cockayne, an Eldorado, a Cloud-Cuckoo-Land, which regrettably or, if you will, fortunately, lasts only one day and the next and then vanishes like a midsummer night's dream, to survive only as a memory and maybe as a hope.

I don't lightly miss taking part in this holiday. I am a passionate lover of my fellow men, and especially of the common people—so much so that even as a dramatist I find the straightforward, if rowdy, response of the public in a packed theater ten times as interesting and indeed as instructive as the excogitated judgment of some literary matador, crippled in body and soul and bloated like a spider with the blood sucked from authors. As a lover of my fellow men, I say, especially when in a crowd they forget their private purposes for a while and feel themselves part of the whole wherein, ultimately, lies the divine, every popular celebration is to me a true spiritual celebration, a pilgrimage, an act of devotion. As though from some vast Plutarch which has escaped from the bounds of the book and lies in an open scroll before me, I read the collective biographies of men unknown to fame. I read them in their faces, cheerful or worried by some secret, in their sprightly or dragging step, in the behavior of members of a family toward each other, in some unpremeditated remark. In truth, no one can understand the lives of the famous unless he has entered into the feelings of the humble. An invisible but continuous thread connects the brawling of drunken market porters with the strife of the sons of the gods, and Juliet, Dido or Medea exist in embryo within every young servant girl who, half against her will, follows her insistent lover out of the dancing crowd.

Two years ago I had, as usual, gone on foot to join the merrymakers at the fair. The main difficulties of the journey had been overcome and I was already at the end of the Augarten, with my longed-for goal, Brigittenau, immediately ahead. At this point one more battle, the last, is still to be fought. A narrow causeway running between impassable enclosures forms the only connection between the two pleasure grounds, whose common boundary is marked midway by a wooden gate. On ordinary days there is more than enough room on this path for the ordinary walker. But during the fair, even were the path four times as wide, it would still be too narrow for the endless crowd which, pushed and pushing vigorously from behind and squeezed in front by those returning in the opposite direction, only manages to sort itself out at all thanks to the universal good humor.

I had abandoned myself to the drifting throng and was in the middle of the causeway, on classical ground already, but, alas, still having to stop again and again, to get out of the way and wait. Thus I had time and to spare to watch what was going on by the roadside.

So that the pleasure-hungry crowd should not lack a foretaste of the delights to come, a number of musicians had stationed themselves to the left, on the slope of the raised causeway; doubtless they were anxious to avoid serious competition and hoped that here, at the temple gates, they might gather the first fruits of the people's as yet unspent generosity. There was a woman harpist with repulsive, glassy eyes. There was an old cripple with a wooden leg, who labored away at a frightful, obviously homemade instrument, half zither and half barrel-organ, to bring home to the general sympathy by due means the aches and pains of his injury. There was a lame, misshapen

boy, hunched inextricably over his fiddle, who played an unending stream of waltzes with all the feverish frenzy of his deformed breast. And finally —he captured my whole attention—there was an old man of at least seventy, in a threadbare but decent overcoat of Molton cloth and with a smiling, self-congratulating expression. He was bareheaded and bald, and, in the way of such people, he had placed his hat on the ground as a collecting box. He sawed away at an old, much cracked violin, and beat time not only by lifting and dropping his foot, but by a corresponding movement of his whole bowed body. Yet all his efforts to give some shape to his performance were fruitless, because what he played seemed nothing but a disjointed sequence of sounds, keeping to no time or tune. For all that, he was utterly absorbed in his task; his lips twitched, his eyes were rigidly fixed on the sheet of music before him—he really did have a piece of music! All the other musicians, whose playing was incomparably more pleasing, relied on their memory, but the old man, in the midst of the throng, had set up a small, easily portable music stand supporting grubby, tattered scores which doubtless contained in perfect order what he rendered in so disordered a fashion. It was precisely the unusual nature of his equipment which drew my attention, just as it aroused the mirth of the passing crowds who made fun of him and left empty his collecting hat, while the rest of the orchestra were bringing in loads of coppers. In order to observe this eccentric undisturbed I had walked a little way off along the slope of the causeway. He went on playing for a while. At last he stopped, and as though recovering his wits after a long trance, he glanced up at the sky which was beginning to show signs of approaching evening, then down at his hat, noticed that it was empty, and with undisturbed cheerfulness put it on and laid the bow between the strings. *"Sunt certi denique fines,"* he said, grabbed his music stand and went off, working his way through the crowd coming to the fair, against the stream, like someone who is going home.

The old man and everything about him were just made to excite my anthropological avidity to the utmost: his needy, though distinguished appearance, his unconquerable cheerfulness combined with so much zeal for his art and so much clumsiness, and the fact that he turned homeward at precisely the hour when others of his kind were just starting on their real harvest, and finally the few words of Latin, pronounced with exactly the right accentuation and complete fluency. So the man had enjoyed a fairly good education, had acquired some learning—and now was a begging, itinerant musician! I was eager for the explanation.

But already there was a dense pack of people between me and him. Small as he was, with his music stand getting in the way all over the place, he was pushed from one person to another, and the exit gate had swallowed him while I was still in the middle of the causeway, struggling against the opposing current of people. So he escaped me, and when I, too, at last got out into the open, there was nowhere any sign of the fiddler.

Cheated of my would-be adventure, I had lost all pleasure in the fair. I wandered about the Augarten in every direction, and finally decided to go home.

As I approached the little gate that leads from the Augarten to Taborstrasse, I suddenly heard once more the familiar sound of the old violin. I hastened my steps, and there before me was the object of my curiosity, playing for all he was worth amid a ring of boys who impatiently demanded a waltz.

"Play a waltz," they cried. "A waltz! Don't you hear?"

The old man fiddled away, apparently unheeding, until his little audience, shouting abuse and derision, left him and collected about an organ-grinder who had set up his barrel-organ nearby.

"They don't want to dance," said the old man, as though cast down, while he gathered up his things. I came up to him, and said: "It's just that the children don't know any dances except the waltz."

"I was playing a waltz," he answered, and pointed with his bow to the music of the piece he had just played. "One has to provide such things, to please the crowd. But the children have no ear," he said, sadly shaking his head.

"Won't you let me make up for their ingratitude," I said, taking a silver coin from my pocket and holding it out to him.

"Please, please!" said the old man, nervously fending it off with his hands. "In the hat, in the hat!"

I placed the coin in the hat that lay before him, from which the old man at once took it and pocketed it with obvious satisfaction. "For once I'll be going home with good takings," he said, chuckling.

"That reminds me," I said, "of something I was already curious about. Your takings today don't seem to have been of the best, and yet you go away just when the crop is ready to be picked. I suppose you know the fair goes on all night, and you could easily earn more then than during a whole week of ordinary days. What's the explanation?"

"What's the explanation?" the old man repeated. "Pardon me, I don't know who you are, though you must be a kind gentleman and a music lover." And he took the coin out of his pocket again and held it between his hands which he raised to his breast. "So I will tell you the reason, even though it often makes people laugh at me. In the first place, I was never given to reveling at night and don't think it right to incite others with music and song to such sinful doings. Secondly, one must maintain a certain order in all things, or else one slides into undisciplined ways, into sheer anarchy. And finally, in the third place—well, sir, all day long I play for the rowdy people and barely make a living out of it, but the evening belongs to me and my poor art. In the evening I stay at home and (he spoke more and more softly, and a blush spread over his face, while he looked at the ground) then I play from imagination, for myself, without a score. Improvising, I believe it's called in music books."

We both fell silent: he from shame at having

given away his inmost secret, and I from astonishment at this reference to the highest level of art from a man who could not give a recognizable rendering of the simplest waltz. Meanwhile, he was getting ready to depart.

"Where do you live?" I said. "I should very much like to join you at your solitary exercises some time."

"Oh," he replied, almost imploringly, "prayer is private, you know."

"Let me call on you during the day, then," I said.

"All day I'm out getting my living," he answered.

"Early in the morning, perhaps?"

"It almost seems," said the old man with a smile, "as though you, my dear sir, were the one to receive a favor and I, if I may presume to say so, were the benefactor. You are so kind and I'm so disagreeable as to retreat into my shell. My abode will be honored to receive such a distinguished visitor at any time. I would only ask that you be so very obliging as to notify me in advance of the day of your advent, so that you will suffer no unseemly loss of time, nor I the inconvenience of having to interrupt whatever I may have begun to do. You see, my mornings are also apportioned. I always consider it my duty to offer my patrons and benefactors some not entirely unworthy return for their gifts. I don't want to be a beggar, my dear sir. Other street musicians, I know, are content to learn by heart a few popular hits, German waltzes, or indeed the tune of some lewd song, and to start over and over again at the same point and play through the whole lot, until people give them something just to get rid of them, or perhaps because the tunes revive the pleasant memory of a dance or some other disorderly diversion. That's why they play from memory, never mind if they get a note wrong every now and then, or indeed often. But so far as I am concerned, far be it from me to cheat. For that reason, I myself made these clean copies of music scores, partly because my memory is not exactly of the best, and partly because it must be difficult for anyone to keep in mind every note of intricate compositions by respected composers."

At that he pointed to his music book and turned over the pages. I was flabbergasted to see compositions by old and famous masters, fantastically difficult and thick with fast runs and double stoppings, all copied out meticulously in a hideous, stiff hand. And this was the sort of thing the old man played with his clumsy fingers!

"By playing these pieces," he went on, "I show my veneration for masters and composers long-since dead and rightly held in high regard. I also satisfy myself and live in the pleasant hope that the offerings most kindly made to me are not left unrequited, thanks to the refining of taste and feeling in a public which otherwise is confused and misled from so many quarters. But as that kind of thing, to come back to what I was saying" —and he smiled with self-satisfaction—"as that kind of thing requires practice, my morning hours are allotted exclusively to this *exercitium*. I think it is no unfair division of my time to give the first three hours of the day to practice, the middle to earning a living, and the evening to myself and God." As he spoke his eyes glistened as though they were moist; but he smiled.

"All right," I said, "I will call on you one of these mornings. Where do you live?"

In Gärtnergasse, he said.

"What number?"

"Number 34, first floor."

"Really," I exclaimed, on the best floor?"

"As a matter of fact," he said, "it's a one-story house, but next to the loft there's a little room which I share with two journeymen."

"Three people in one room?"

"It's divided up and I have my own bed."

"It's getting late," I said, "and you want to go home. So good-bye, and we'll meet again."

I felt in my pocket for a coin to double what little I had given him before. But he had picked up his music stand with one hand and his violin with the other, and said hastily:

"With your permission—no. I have already received an ample honorarium for my playing, and I'm not conscious of having rendered any other service so far."

At that he bowed to me in an awkward imitation of elegant ease and departed as quickly as his old legs would carry him.

As I have mentioned, I had lost any desire to spend more time at the fair that day, and so I turned homeward, taking the road to Leopoldstadt. Weary with dust and heat, I entered one of the many local inns, where the garden is packed on ordinary days, but which today had lost all its customers to Brigittenau. The quiet of the place, far from the madding crowd, was a relief to me. I was so lost in my reflections, in which the old fiddler had no small part, that night had fully come before I at last thought of going home, put the money for my bill on the table, and stepped out toward the city.

The old man had said he lived in Gärtnergasse. I asked a small boy who was running past: "Is Gärtnergasse around here?"

"That way, mister," he replied, and pointed to a side street which led away from the suburban cluster of houses toward the open country. I went in that direction. The road consisted of dispersed, individual houses situated among large market gardens, which plainly indicated both the occupation of the inhabitants and the origin of the name "Gardeners' Lane." In which of these poor cottages, I wondered, did my eccentric live? I had cheerfully forgotten the house number, and anyway, in the dark there was not much chance of making out a sign. A man heavily laden with garden produce came toward me. "The old man's scraping away again," he said as he passed, "spoiling everyone's peace and quiet."

At the same time, as I went on, my ear caught the soft, long-drawn note of a violin; it seemed to issue from the open loft window of a poorish-looking house not far away. Like the rest of them it was low and without an upper story, but it differed from the others in having this window in the gable under the eaves. I stood still. A note, soft, yet firmly struck, swelled to the point of violence, faded and died away, only to rise again to a piercing shrillness. It was always the same note, repeated with a sort of voluptuous insistence. At last the player sounded an interval. It was a fourth. While at first he had dwelt on the single note with manifest relish, his almost sensual enjoyment of the harmonic relationship struck me with even greater force. He sounded the two notes now successively, now as a chord, haltingly linked them by the intervening scale, emphasized the third, again and again. Then a fifth was added, once with a trembling sound, like quiet weeping, sustained, dying away, then with rushing impetuosity, continually repeated, always the same interval, the same notes. And this was what the old man called improvisation! It was, I suppose, improvising after a fashion, but for the benefit of the performer only, not of the listener.

I do not know how long it may have lasted, nor how bad it had been. Suddenly the door of the house opened and a man wearing only a shirt and loosely fastened trousers came out into the middle of the road and shouted up to the gable window: "Aren't you ever going to stop today, either?" His voice sounded annoyed, but not harsh or insulting. The violin fell silent before the man had finished speaking. He went back into the house, the gable window was closed, and soon there was unbroken silence all about me. I set out for home, finding my way with difficulty through the unfamiliar lanes, and also improvising—in my mind, without disturbing anyone.

For me the morning hours have always possessed a special value. I seem to feel a need to sanctify, as it were, the rest of the day by devoting its first hours to something significant, something inspiring. So I find it difficult to leave my room in the early morning, and if I force myself to do so without good cause, then all day long I have the choice only between unthinking distraction and self-tormenting gloom. Thus it was that for several days I postponed my visit to the old man, which it had been agreed should take place in the morning. At last impatience got the better of me, and I went. I easily found Gärtnergasse and the house. Once again the notes of the violin could be heard, but this time muffled and indistinguishable because the window was closed. I entered the house. The gardener's wife, almost speechless with surprise, showed me up the stairs to the loft. There I found myself at a low, badly fitting door. I knocked and, getting no answer, at last turned the handle and went in. The room was fairly large, but otherwise as miserable as could be, and its walls sloped with the steep pitch of the roof. Close to the door was a disgustingly dirty, tousled bed, surrounded by all the appurtenances of slovenliness. Opposite, hard by the narrow window, was another bed, poor, but clean and most carefully made and

covered. By the window a small table with music paper and writing materials, and in the window a few pots of flowers. The middle of the room was marked by a broad chalk line from wall to wall. One could hardly imagine a sharper contrast between dirt and cleanliness than the aspect of the nearer and farther sides of the chalk line, this equator of a miniature world.

The old man had placed his music stand close to the line, and there he stood, fully and neatly dressed, and practiced. So much has been said already, to the point of dissonance, about the cacophonies of this favorite character of mine (and, I almost fear, only mine), that I will spare the reader a description of this infernal concert. As his practice consisted mainly of passage work, there was no hope of recognizing the pieces he played, which in any case would hardly have been easy. After listening for a while I at last found the thread through the labyrinth, the method in his madness. The old man found a sensuous enjoyment in playing. In his conception, there was only one distinction that mattered: consonance and dissonance. The former pleased, indeed delighted him, while the latter, even if harmonically justified, he avoided so far as possible. Therefore, instead of bringing out the sense and rhythm of a piece, he emphasized and prolonged the notes and intervals which struck mellifluously upon the ear, and did not hesitate to repeat them arbitrarily, his face often expressing utter ecstasy as he did so. As he skipped over the dissonances as quickly as possible, and, too conscientious to miss a single note, slowed down disproportionately in passages which were too difficult for him, it is easy to form an idea of the confusion which emerged from it all. At last, even I could stand it no longer.

After unsuccessfully trying various ways of recalling him to his whereabouts, I deliberately dropped my hat. The old man was startled, his knees trembled, he could hardly keep hold of the violin which sank to the floor. I stepped forward.

"Oh, it's you, my dear sir!" he said, recovering his wits. "I had not reckoned with your gracious promise being fulfilled."

He urged me to be seated, cleared up, put things away, looked about the room several times, as though embarrassed, then abruptly picked up a plate from a table near the door and went out. I heard him talking to the gardener's wife outside. Soon he came back, still embarrassed, and holding behind his back the plate which he surreptitiously put down again. Obviously he had asked for some fruit to offer me, but had not managed to get it.

"It's nice here," I said, to relieve his embarrassment. "Disorder is banished. It retreats toward the door, even though it has not yet quite crossed the threshold."

"My place only goes as far as the mark," said the old man, pointing to the chalk line through the middle of the room. "Over there live a couple of journeymen."

"And do they respect this mark of yours?"

"They don't, but I do," he said. "Only the door is in common."

"And aren't you disturbed by your neighbors?"

"Hardly," he said. "They come home late at night, and if they do wake me when I'm in bed, that only makes it all the more enjoyable to fall asleep again. But in the morning it's I who wake them up, when I tidy my room. Then they curse a bit, and go out."

In the meanwhile I had been observing him. He was very neatly dressed and his figure was not at all bad for his years, except that his legs were a bit short. His hands and feet were remarkably finely formed.

"You're looking at me," he said. "A penny for your thoughts?"

"I'm curious to know your story," I replied.

"My story?" he repeated, "I have no story. Today is the same as yesterday, and tomorrow as today. As for the day after tomorrow and beyond, who can tell? But God will provide, he knows."

"I daresay your life now is monotonous," I continued, "but your fortunes in earlier days? How it happened. . . . "

". . . that I became a street musician?" he

intervened in the pause I had involuntarily made. So I told him how he had caught my attention at once when I first saw him, of the impression his few words of Latin had made on me.

"Latin," he picked on the word. "Ah yes, Latin, that is indeed something I learnt once, or rather should and could have learnt. *Loqueris latine?*" he asked, addressing me, "but I could not continue. It is too long ago. So that's what you call my story? How it all came about? Well yes, all sorts of things did happen; nothing very special, but quite a lot anyway. I wouldn't mind recalling it all, for my own sake. Just to make sure I haven't forgotten. It is early yet," he continued, reaching for his watch pocket, in which, alas, he found no watch.

I pulled out my own. It was barely nine o'clock.

"We have plenty of time, and I almost feel tempted to reminisce a bit."

While he said this, I could see him relaxing. He straightened himself up. Without too much ceremony he relieved me of my hat and put it on the bed, sat down with his legs crossed and altogether adopted the attitude of one who is going to talk at his leisure.

"No doubt," he began, "you have heard of *Hofrat*—?"

The name was that of a well-known political figure who had exercised enormous influence, almost as much as a minister, during the second half of the last century, although officially he was only a civil servant of modest rank. I confirmed that I knew of the man.

"He was my father," he continued.

His father? An old fiddler, a beggar—and this man of power and influence was his father? The old man did not seem to notice my surprise, but, visibly pleased, went on spinning his yarn.

"I was the second of three brothers. Both the others climbed high in government service, but are now dead; I'm the only one still living," he said, and, with eyes cast down, plucked at his threadbare trousers and picked off a little piece of fluff.

"My father was an ambitious and violent man. My brothers lived up to his expectations, but as for me, people used to say I was slow in the uptake. And I was slow. If my memory doesn't betray me"—and turning sideways, as though gazing into the far distance, he leaned his head on his left hand—"If my memory doesn't betray me, I would have been quite capable of learning all sorts of things, if only I had been given time and a chance of orderly progress. My brothers leapt about like chamois from the summit of one subject to the next, but I could never skip anything at all, and if I missed a single word, I had to start again from the beginning. So I was always being pushed. New things were to take the place not yet vacated by old ones, and I became a refractory child. Music, for instance, which is now the joy and staff of my life, was made utterly hateful to me. When I took up my violin in the evening twilight to amuse myself after my own fashion by playing without a score, they would take the instrument from me, saying that this would ruin my fingering, complaining that it was torture for their ears and telling me to wait for my music lesson—when it was my turn to endure torture. All my life I have never hated anything or anybody as much as I hated the violin at that time.

"Thoroughly disappointed with me, my father often upbraided me and threatened to apprentice me to some manual trade. I didn't dare to say how happy this would have made me. I would have liked nothing better than to become a turner or a compositor. But he wouldn't have let me, anyway, it would have hurt his pride. The last straw was a public examination at school. In an effort to placate him, they had persuaded my father to attend; the disingenuous teacher had told me in advance what he was going to ask me, and so everything went swimmingly. I had to recite from memory some verses of Horace; suddenly, toward the end, there was one word I couldn't think of. My teacher had nodded his head and smiled at my father while he listened to me; now, as I was stuck, he tried to rescue me by whispering the word. But I was searching for the word within myself and the overall context, and did not hear him. He repeated it several times, all in vain. At last my father lost his patience. *Cacchinum*—that was the word—he yelled at me. That was my final undoing. Knowing that one word, I forgot all the rest. Every attempt to get me back onto the right track failed. I had to withdraw ignominiously, and when, as was the custom, I went to kiss my father's hand, he pushed me aside, got up, bowed briefly to the company and left. *Ce gueux,* he scornfully called me—which I wasn't then, but am now. There's prophesy in what parents say! For the rest, my father was not a wicked man, only violent and ambitious.

"From this day onward he never addressed another word to me. His orders were transmitted to me by other members of the household. The very next day I was told that there was to be an end to my studying. I was greatly upset, because I knew what a bitter hurt this must be for my father. All day long I did nothing but cry and in between recite those Latin verses, which I now remembered down to the last syllable, and the preceding and following ones, to boot. I promised to make good my lack of talent by hard work, if only I were allowed to go on with school. But my father never revoked a decision.

"For some time I remained in my father's house without anything to do. Eventually I was placed in an accounts office, on trial. But I had never been any good at figures. The suggestion that I should join the army I rejected with horror. To this day I cannot look at a uniform without an inward shudder. To protect one's kith and kin, if need be at the risk of one's life, well and good; but to choose bloodshed and butchery as a calling, as an occupation—no! Never, never!"

He passed both hands over both arms, as if in pain from his own and other people's wounds.

"Finally they made me a copy clerk in the chancery. That was just the place for me. I had always enjoyed writing, and to this day I know of no more agreeable diversion than to take some good ink and good paper, and join thin stroke to thick stroke to form words, or even just single letters. Music notes are especially beautiful. But at that time I had as yet no thought of music.

"I worked hard, but I was too timid. One wrong punctuation mark, one illegible word or one missing from the draft, even if it could easily be guessed from the context, caused me hours of perplexity. Uncertain whether to stick precisely to the original or to add something on my own responsibility, I would timorously let the time pass, and so I got a reputation for slackness, even though I took more pains than anyone else. A few years went by in this way, and I still got no pay, because when I was due for promotion, my father cast his vote in the council for someone else and the others concurred in deference to him.

"Around that time"—and suddenly the old man interrupted himself—"who would have thought so? It is a sort of story after all! All right, let us tell the story, then.

"Around that time two events came to pass, the saddest and the gladdest of my life. I mean my leaving my father's house and my return to my beloved music, to my violin, which has remained faithful to me to this day.

"I lived in my father's house, but no one took

any notice of me. I had a back room, overlooking the neighbor's yard. At first, I used to join the family at meals, when no one said a single word to me. Then my brothers got promoted and went away, and my father was invited out nearly every day—my mother was long dead—and so it was found inconvenient to have to cook just for me. The servants were given money for their board, and so was I, except that the cash was not handed over to me, put paid every month directly to a chophouse. So I didn't spend much time in my room, save in the evening, for my father required me to be home not later than half an hour after the office closed. I used to sit there in the dusk, without light, because of my eyes which were weak even then. I thought of this and that, and was neither sad nor happy.

"Sitting there, I would hear someone sing a song in the neighbor's yard—or rather several songs, but there was one which I liked especially. It was such a simple, such a moving song with just the right lilt, so that there was no need at all to hear the words. Besides, in my view, words only spoil music anyway."

He opened his mouth and produced a few hoarse, raw sounds.

"I never had a singing voice," he said, and reached for his violin. He played, this time with correct expression, a tune which was pleasant enough, but by no means outstanding. His fingers were shaking on the strings, and soon a few tears trickled down his cheeks.

"That was the song," he said, putting down the violin. "It gave me new pleasure every time I heard it. But however vivid it remained in my memory, I never managed to reproduce as much as two notes of it correctly by voice. I fretted impatiently from just listening. But once, suddenly, my eye fell upon my violin. This relic of my childhood days was hanging on the wall, unused, like an old piece of armor. I took it down and, strangely enough, found it properly tuned; maybe a servant had used it in my absence. As I now swept over the strings with my bow, it was as if God's finger had touched me. The sound penetrated my inmost being and thence issued forth again. The air around me was as if pregnant with ecstasy. Down below in the yard the song, and close to my ear the sounds I made with my fingers —they came to dwell with me in my loneliness. I fell upon my knees and prayed aloud, and could not understand how I had ever, as a child, belittled and indeed hated this divine beauty, and I kissed the violin and pressed it to my heart and played again and again.

"The song in the yard—it was sung by a woman's voice—meanwhile went on ceaselessly; but I did not find it so easy to play.

"I had no score for the song, you see. Furthermore, I realized that I had all but forgotten what little I ever knew of the art of fiddling. For that reason I was able to play not any particular piece or other, but simply to play, as such. I should add, though, that with the sole exception of that song, I always was rather indifferent to the specific content of any piece of music, and still am. They play Wolfgang Amadeus Mozart and Johann Sebastian Bach, but no one plays God. The eternal boon and grace of sound and tone, their miraculous consort with the thirsting, parched ear, the way the third note"—he continued more softly, blushing with shame—"the way the third accords with the first and with the fifth also, and the *nota sensibilis* soars like hope fulfilled while dissonance is humbled like purposed evil or overweening pride, the miracle of ligature and inversion, whereby even the second attains to grace in the womb of harmony. A musician explained all that to me, much later however. And there are yet other matters, of which

I understand nothing, like the fugue and counterpoint and the two- or three-part canon, and so forth—the whole heavenly edifice, each piece interlocking with the other, joined together without mortar, held in God's hand. But no one cares about these things except a very few. Instead they disturb the ebb and flow of the soul's breathing by adding, maybe, the spoken word, just as the sons of God united with the daughters of earth, thus nicely invading and pervading the callous heart. Sir," he concluded, almost exhausted, "speech is as necessary to man as food, but he should also keep pure the spring that comes from God."

I hardly recognized the man, he had become so worked up. He paused for a moment.

"But where had I got to in my story?" he said at last. "Ah yes, to the song and to my attempts to play it. I simply could not do it. I stepped closer to the window in order to hear better. Just then the singer crossed the yard. I saw only her back, and yet she looked familiar to me. She was carrying what seemed to be a basket of unbaked cakes. She went in through a little door at the corner of the yard, to where there was an oven, perhaps, for I could hear a scraping of wooden implements; she continued singing, but her voice sounded first duller and then clearer, as though its owner were bending down and singing into a cavity, and then standing up straight again. After a while she came back, and then I realized why she had seemed familiar to me. I had indeed known her for some time. From the office, as a matter of fact.

"What had happened was this. We used to start work early and go on beyond midday. Several of the younger clerks were in the habit of taking a snack around eleven o'clock, either because they really were hungry or as a means of filling in half an hour. The tradespeople, who know how to turn everything to their own advantage, saved our epicures the trouble of going out. They brought their wares to the office building and stationed themselves along the staircase and corridors. There was a baker selling small white rolls, a greengrocer woman with cherries. One of the most popular items was a certain type of cake, which a neighboring grocer's daughter used to bake herself and offer for sale still warm from the oven. Her customers usually stepped out into the corridor to buy from her and only rarely, when she was called, did she enter the room itself. It was equally rare for our rather ill-tempered head clerk not to send her away again as soon as he noticed her. She would comply unwillingly, muttering indignantly under her breath.

"My colleagues did not consider the girl pretty. They thought she was too short, the color of her hair too mousy. Some denied that she had green eyes, but all agreed about her pockmarks. The one feature everyone praised was her strapping figure, though they thought she was rough and one of them was always talking about how she'd boxed his ears so soundly that it had hurt for a week—or so he claimed.

"I myself was not one of her customers. First of all I had no money, and secondly food and drink was, no doubt, something I always had to accept as a necessity, and sometimes only too much so, but which I never dreamed of regarding as a source of pleasure and enjoyment. So we took no notice of one another. Only once, to tease me, one of my colleagues led her to believe that I had asked for her cakes. She stepped up to my table and proffered her basket.

" 'I don't want to buy anything, thank you, miss,' I said.

" 'Well, in that case, why do you trouble people to come?' she exclaimed crossly.

"I apologized, and since I realized at once that

it was a practical joke, I explained matters to her as best I could.

" 'If that's so,' she said, 'at least give me a sheet of paper to put my cakes on.'

"I made it clear that this was office paper and did not belong to me, but added that I had paper of my own at home and would gladly bring her some of that.

" 'At home I have enough myself,' she mocked, and laughed briefly as she left.

"This had happened only a few days ago and now I thought I could satisfy my wish at once by means of this acquaintance. The very next morning I took a whole quire of paper, of which there was never any lack in our house, and stuffed it under my jacket when I went to the office. So as not to give myself away, I kept my highly uncomfortable armor on until, in the late morning, the coming and going of my colleagues and the sound of champing jaws told me that the pastry-vendor had come. When I thought the main crush of business was over, I went outside, pulled out my paper, took my courage in both hands and approached the girl. She had placed her basket in front of herself on the floor, and, standing with her right foot on the stool on which she usually sat, sang softly while she beat time with the foot that rested on the stool. As I approached, she looked me up and down from top to toe, which did nothing to diminish my embarrassment.

" 'My dear young lady,' I eventually began, 'the other day you asked me for paper, when I had none of my own to hand. Now I have brought you some from home and. . . .' I held out my paper to her.

" 'I told you then that I had plenty at home,' she said. 'However, I suppose it might come in useful.'

"With these words and a slight nod of the head, she took my gift and put it in her basket.

" 'You don't want any of my cakes, do you?' she said, fingering her wares. 'In any case, the best have gone.'

"I said, No thank you, but that I had another request.

" 'And what might that be?' she said. She quickly pushed her arm through the handle of her basket, stood up straight and eyed me fiercely.

"Hastily I blurted out that I was a lover of music, though only a recent one, and that I had heard her sing such lovely songs, one in particular.

" 'You? Me? Songs?' she rejoined. 'And where?'

"I told her then that I lived near her and had

overheard her in the yard, at work. One of her songs I liked so much that I had already tried to play it on the violin.

" 'So you're the one,' she exclaimed, 'who scrapes away on the fiddle?'

"I was but a beginner at that time, as I mentioned before. It was only later and with a lot of trouble that I acquired the necessary fluency of the fingers," the old man interrupted himself, while he fingered about in the air with his left hand, as if fiddling.

"The blood had rushed to my face," he said, picking up his tale again, "and I looked at her and saw that she was sorry for her harsh words. 'Young lady,' I said, 'if I scrape, it's because I don't have the score of the song, and that is why, with your permission, I'd ask you for a copy of it.'

" 'A copy?' she said, 'but the song is in print and you can buy it at any street corner.'

" 'The song?' I replied, 'surely, only the words.'

" 'Well yes, the words, the song.'

" 'But what about the tune, what you sing, I mean?'

" 'Oh, is that kind of thing written down too?' she asked.

" 'Of course,' I answered, 'that's the main thing. How indeed did you ever learn it?'

" 'I heard it sung, so I repeated it by ear.'

"I marveled at this natural talent. It often happens that the uneducated are the most gifted. Nevertheless, this is not the real thing, not true art. I was in despair again.

" 'What song do you mean, anyway?' she asked. 'I know so many.'

" 'All without a score?'

" 'Of course. Which one was it, then?'

" 'It's a wonderful one,' I explained. 'It soars right at the beginning, then turns back upon itself and ends quite softly. Also, it's the one you sing most often.'

" 'Ah, I know, this'll be the one,' she said, put down her basket again and, with a soft but clear voice, sang the song. She bent her head as she sang, and it was so sweet and lovely that I reached out for her hand before she had even finished.

" 'Take it easy,' she said, pulling back her arm. No doubt she thought I was making a pass at her, but I merely wanted to kiss her hand, even though she was but a poor girl. Well, now I, too, am a poor man.

"Desperate to possess the song, I was tearing

my hair. When she saw this she comforted me, and said the organist of St. Peter's often came for nutmeg to her father's store, and she would ask him to write it all down for me. I could collect it there in a few days' time.

"Thereupon she picked up her basket and went. I accompanied her as far as the staircase, but just as I was taking final leave of her at the top of the stairs, the head clerk suddenly appeared and ordered me back to my work. As for the girl, he had harsh words for her and said she was a good-for-nothing. I was furious and was just about to retort that, with his permission, I was convinced of the contrary. But he had already returned to his room, and so I pulled myself together and also went back to my desk. After that, however, he could not be dissuaded from considering me a negligent clerk and generally a dissolute young man.

"As a matter of fact I was hardly able to do any decent work at all that day and the following days. My mind was so full of the song that I went about in a dream. A few days passed, but I couldn't make up my mind whether or not it was time to go and fetch the music. The organist, the girl had said, came to her father's store to buy nutmeg. All he could use that for was beer. Now, the weather had been cool for some time and there was every likelihood that the worthy instrumentalist would stick to wine and wouldn't need any nutmeg so soon. To inquire too quickly seemed discourteous and forward, while to wait too long might be interpreted as indifference. To speak to the girl in the corridor was more than I dared, for our first encounter had begun to be talked about among my colleagues and they were itching to make mischief.

"Meanwhile I had taken up the violin again with passion. For the time being I practiced thoroughly the basic essentials, though every now and then I indulged in some improvisation, always carefully closing the window, because I knew that my performance wasn't liked. But even when I opened the window, I never heard my song again. My neighbor either sang it not at all, or so softly or behind closed doors, that I could not distinguish as much as two notes.

"Finally, after about three weeks had passed, I could stand it no longer. Twice already, in the evening, I had crept through the house, hatless, so that the servants should think I was merely looking for something, and out into the street. But whenever I came near the grocer's shop I was overcome by such violent trembling that, willy-nilly, I had to turn back. At last, as I said, I could stand it no longer. I took my courage in both hands and one evening, again hatless, I walked down the stairs from my room and firmly strode along the street right up to the grocer's shop. There I

paused and took thought as to what to do next. The shop was lighted, and I heard voices inside. After some hesitation I bent forward and peeped in from the side. I saw the girl sitting close to the counter near the lamp, picking over peas and beans in a wooden bowl. In front of her stood a rough, sturdy man, his jacket slung over his shoulder and a sort of cudgel in his hand, rather like a butcher. They were talking, obviously in high spirits, for the girl laughed out aloud every now and then, without, however, interrupting her work or even looking up. Whether it was because of my awkward, bent posture or for some other reason, I began trembling again. Suddenly I was grabbed rudely from behind and dragged forward. In no time I was inside and when I was let go, I looked round and saw that it was the owner himself who on returning home had caught me peering in, suspiciously as it seemed, and had seized me.

" 'What the dickens!' he shouted, 'Now we know where the prunes get to, and the handfuls of peas and pearl barley pinched from the display baskets in the dark. Damnation strike you dead!' And at that he made for me as if indeed to strike me.

"I felt annihilated, but the idea that my honesty was being questioned soon restored my wits. I bowed curtly and informed the boor that my visit had nothing to do with his prunes or his barley, but with his daughter. Thereupon the butcher burst into a loud guffaw and turned to go, not before whispering a few words to the girl. She responded, also laughing, by giving him a resounding slap on the back with her hand. The grocer accompanied the departing visitor out of the door.

Meanwhile I had lost all my courage once more and stood there, facing the girl, who went on picking out her peas and beans with unconcern, as if the whole thing was no business of hers. Presently the father stumped back through the door.

" 'God damn it all!' he said, 'What's all this about my daughter?'

"I tried to explain the whole matter and why I had come to call.

" 'Song indeed!' he cried, 'You wait and I'll sing you a song!' He was swinging his right arm most ominously.

" 'It's over there,' the girl said, tilting sideways, chair and all, without putting down her bowl, and pointing to the counter. I rushed over and saw a sheet of music. It was the song. But the old chap had got there first. He grabbed the beautiful paper and crumpled it.

" 'I want to know,' he said, 'what all this is about? Who is this man?'

" 'He is a gentleman from the chancery office,' she replied, throwing a maggoty pea farther away than the others.

" 'A gentleman from the chancery office?' he said, 'In the dark? Without a hat?'

"I explained the absence of a hat by the circumstance that I lived quite near, and identified the house.

" 'I know the house,' he cried. 'No one lives there but *Hofrat*—,' he said, naming my father. 'And I know every one of the servants.'

" 'I am the *Hofrat*'s son,' I said, softly, as if it were a lie.

"I've seen many a transformation in my life, but none so abrupt as that which my words caused in the man's whole attitude. His mouth, open already for new vituperations, hung wide open, the eyes still glowered, but around the lower part of his face a kind of smile began to flicker up and to gain ground. The girl maintained her indifference and her bowed head, except that, still working on, she smoothed some loose hairs back behind her ear.

" 'The *Herr Hofrat*'s son!' the old man exclaimed at last, his face now quite clear. 'Won't your honor be seated? Barbara, a chair!'

"The girl shifted uneasily on her own chair.

" 'All right, you old slyboots,' he said, himself lifting a basket off a chair and wiping the dust from the latter with his apron.

" 'What an honor,' he continued. 'So *Herr Hofrat,* I mean, the young master, is also a practitioner of music? He sings, perhaps, like my girl, or rather not like her, but properly according to the rules of the art, from written music?'

"I explained that nature had not favored me with a singing voice.

" 'You play the clavicembalo, perhaps, as the gentry often do?'

"I said I played the violin.

" 'I used to scrape away at a fiddle, too, when I was young,' he cried.

"At the word scrape I couldn't help looking at the girl and saw that she was smiling derisively, which vexed me very much.

" 'You should take an interest in the girl—I mean, so far as music is concerned,' he continued. 'She has a pretty voice, and other virtues, but refinement—oh dear, where's that to come from?' and he rubbed his thumb and forefinger together repeatedly.

"I was embarrassed at having such considerable musical accomplishments imputed to me quite undeservedly. I was just about to explain how matters really stood, when a passer-by called in from outside: 'Good evening, everybody!'

"I winced, for I had recognized the voice of one of our servants. The grocer recognized it, too. He put out the tip of his tongue, raised his shoulders and whispered:

" 'It's one of the servants of your honor's papa. But he couldn't see who you were, you were standing with your back to the door.'

"The latter was true enough, but I had a painful sense of hiding something, of being in the wrong. I stammered a few words to take my leave and went away. I would even have left my song behind, if the old man had not run after me into the street and thrust it into my hand.

"Thus I got home, to my room, and waited for further developments. They did not fail to come. The servant had recognized me after all. A few days later my father's secretary came up to my room and informed me that I was to leave home. All protests were in vain. A little room had been rented for me in an outlying suburb, and so I was completely banished from my family. Nor did I set eyes again on my singer. She had been forbidden to sell her cakes at the office, and I could not make up my mind to call at her father's store, because I knew that this would arouse my father's disapproval. Once, when I met the old grocer by chance in the street, he turned away scornfully; I was dumbfounded. Left to myself half the day long, I took up my violin and played and practiced.

"But worse was to come. Our family's fortunes declined. My younger brother, a willful impetuous man, who was an officer in the dragoons, lost his life in a reckless wager. All hot from a ride he went and swam the Danube—it was away down in Hungary—with his horse and arms. The oldest, my favorite brother, had a post on a provincial council. He was continually opposing the regional governor, they said with the surreptitious encouragement of my father, and eventually went so far as to make false statements to discredit his opponent. An inquiry was held, and my brother secretly left the country. My father's enemies, and he had many, seized upon this opportunity to bring about his downfall. Attacked on all sides and embittered by his loss of influence, he took to making the most aggressive speeches every day at the council. Right in the middle of one of them he had a stroke. He was taken home, unable to speak. However, I heard nothing about it all. Next day at the office I did, indeed, notice that people were whispering among themselves and pointing at me. But I was used to that kind of thing and thought nothing of it. It had happened on a Wednesday; on the following Friday, suddenly a black suit and crape were brought to my room. Startled, I put questions and got the answer. I'm usually strong and physically resistant, but now I was completely overcome. I collapsed on the floor, unconscious. They put me to bed, where I raved in a high fever all day and all night. By the next morning, nature had won through, but my father was dead and buried.

"I had been unable to speak to him any more, unable to beg his forgiveness for all the distress I had caused him, unable to thank him for the indulgence I had not deserved—yes, indulgence, because he meant well, and I hope to meet him again in the hereafter, when we shall be judged by our intentions and not by our works.

"I remained in my room for some days, hardly taking any food. At last I went out, but returned immediately after lunch. Only in the evening I roamed about the darkened streets like Cain, the fratricide. My father's house was like a nightmare to me and I took every possible care to avoid it. Once, staring absent-mindedly at nothing at all, I suddenly found myself in the neighborhood of the dreaded house. My knees trembled so violently that I had to lean against the nearest wall. Groping behind me with my hand, I found the door of the grocer's shop. Inside, I saw Barbara, holding a letter, and next to her the lamp on the counter and close by, standing, her father who seemed to be talking at her. I felt that even at the cost of my life I simply had to go in! To have no one to speak to of one's misery, no one who feels any sympathy! The old man, I knew, was incensed against me, but the girl might have a kind word for me. But it all happened the other way round. Barbara got up when I entered, gave me a contemptuous look and went into the room next door, closing the door behind her. The old man, however, took me by the hand, made me sit down and comforted me. At the same time he also conjectured that I was now a rich man and wouldn't need to bother about other people any more. He asked how much I had inherited. I did not know. He urged me to go to the law-courts, and I promised to do so. There was no future in office work, he said, I should invest my inheritance in commerce. Gallnuts and dried fruit were profitable lines, and, given a partner who knew the business, pennies could easily be turned into pounds. He himself had quite a lot of experience with this sort of thing, he assured me.

"He called out repeatedly to the girl, who, however, gave no sign of life. It did seem to me, though, as if I heard a rustle behind the door every now and then. But since she did not reappear and the old man went on talking only about money, I eventually said good-bye and left, amid protestations of regret on the part of the grocer, that he could not accompany me since he was alone in the shop. I was sad at my frustrated hope and yet felt wonderfully comforted. As I stopped in the street and looked across at my father's house, I suddenly heard a voice behind me, low and in a tone of indignation:

" 'Don't trust just anybody. There are some who have designs upon you.'

"Quickly as I turned round, I saw no one. Only the clatter of a window on the ground floor of the grocer's told me, even if I had not recognized her voice, that it was Barbara who had secretly warned me. So she had heard after all what had been spoken in the shop. Did she mean to warn me against her father? Or had it come to her notice that immediately after my father's death some office colleagues, and complete strangers as well, had approached me with requests for help and support, which I had promised, as soon as I came into some money. What promises I had made, I must keep, of course, but I decided to be a little more careful in the future.

"I took steps to claim my inheritance. It was less than had been thought, but still a great deal, close on eleven thousand florins. All day my room was never free of supplicants and people wanting help. But I had become almost hard-hearted and gave only to those whose need was greatest. Barbara's father came, too. He complained that I hadn't shown up for three whole days, to which I replied, quite truthfully, that I was afraid of being unwelcome to his daughter. Never mind about that, he said, he'd given her a good talking to—and he gave a nasty laugh, which shocked me. This reminded me of Barbara's warning, and when presently we came to speak of my inheritance, I was careful not to reveal how much it was, and I also skillfully evaded his business propositions.

"As it happened, I was already making different plans. I had lost my job to someone else at the office, where I had been tolerated only because of my father. As I got no salary there anyway, I didn't mind. But my father's secretary, who now no longer had a job, came to me with a scheme for setting up an information, copying and translation agency for which I was to advance the initial installation costs, whereas he would be willing to take over the management. At my insistence, the copying side of the business was extended to music, and now I was as happy as could be. I provided the necessary money, but, cautious as I was by now, demanded and got a handwritten receipt. The surety that had to be deposited for the agency was high, but caused me no worry, since it was, after all, deposited with the courts and remained as safe as if I had kept it in my own cupboard.

"The matter was settled, and I felt relieved, exalted, for the first time in my life independent, a man at last. I hardly thought of my father any more. I moved into a better apartment, made some changes in my dress and, one evening, I walked through the familiar streets to the grocer's shop, stepping out gaily and humming my song, though not quite correctly. With my voice, I never could hit the B flat in the second half. I arrived in high spirits, but an icy look of Barbara's at once plunged me back into my old timidity. Her father made me welcome, but she behaved as if no one were present, went on twisting paper bags and took no part at all in our conversation. Only when we came to talk of my inheritance, she half started up and said in an almost threatening voice: 'Father!'—whereupon he at once changed the subject. Apart from that she did not say a single word all the evening, never looked at me again, and when at last I took my leave, her 'Good evening' almost sounded like 'Thank God!'

"But I came again and again, and gradually

she softened. Not that I ever managed to please her by anything I did. She constantly scolded and nagged me. She said I was clumsy; that my fingers were all thumbs; my jacket made me look like a scarecrow; that I walked like a duck trying to be cock of the roost. She particularly objected to my obsequiousness to customers. As I had nothing to do until the copying agency got going and thought that, when it did, I would have to deal with the public, I had taken to working fairly regularly in the grocer's shop. I thought retail selling would be good practice, and often stayed half the day. I weighed spices, counted out nuts and prunes for the boys, gave people their change. With this I often made a mistake, and then Barbara invariably intervened, grabbing from me whatever I might have in my hand and laughing at me and mocking me in front of the customers. If I bowed to a customer and presented my compliments, she'd say curtly, before the people were out of the shop, 'The goods speak for themselves,' and turn her back on me. At other times she would be kindness itself. On such occasions she listened when I told her the latest about local town affairs, or about my childhood, or about the ways of officialdom in the chancery office, where we first met. But she always let me soliloquize, saying only a few words now and then to express her approval or, more often, her disapproval.

"Nothing was ever said about music or singing. First of all, she held that one should either sing or keep one's trap shut; there was nothing to talk about. But there was no opportunity for singing. In the shop it would have been out of place, and I was not allowed in the back room, which she shared with her father. Once, when I arrived unnoticed, she was standing on her toes, with her back to me and stretching up her arms, groping for something on one of the higher shelves and singing softly to herself. It was the song, my own song! And there she was, twittering away like a songbird preening its throat by a stream and turning its head this way and that and ruffling its feathers and smoothing them again with its beak. I felt as if I were walking through green fields. I crept up closer and closer until I was so near that the song no longer seemed to come from outside but from right inside me, a song of my own soul. I could not resist: as she was standing there bent over backward, reaching up while her shoulders arched down towards me, with both hands I seized her waist. The reaction was instantaneous. She whirled round like a top, her face flushed with anger, and her hand flew up before I could say a word of excuse—

"I told you earlier about the story at the office, about how Barbara, when she was still selling cakes there, had once slapped an importunate admirer's face. What they said about the strength of the girl, who was really rather small, and the weight of her hand, had seemed grossly exaggerated, just for the fun of it. But it was true, all right, there was something gigantic about it. I felt as though stunned, and lights danced before my eyes. But they were lights of heaven, like the sun, the moon and the stars, like angels playing hide-and-seek and singing all the while. I had visions, I was in a trance. In her turn, she was hardly less startled than myself and, soothing my cheek softly where she'd hit it, said: 'Oh, it was too hard, maybe.' And, as if lightning struck for the second time, I suddenly felt her warm breath on my cheek and a pair of lips: she kissed me, lightly, lightly—but still, it was a kiss, on my cheek, here!

The old man patted his cheek, and tears welled up in his eyes.

"What happened then, I don't know," he continued. "The only thing I remember is that I rushed at her and she fled into the living room and

held the glass door closed, while I pushed at it from outside. Almost doubled up with the effort of holding fast, she had her face practically glued to the windowpane, and I, dear sir, I summoned up my courage and passionately returned her kiss, through the glass.

" 'Well, well, what fun and games!' I suddenly heard a voice behind me. It was the grocer who had come home. 'It's just a lovers' tiff. Come on out, Barb, don't be silly. There's nothing amiss in an honest kiss.'

"But she did not come. And I left after stuttering a few incoherent words. In my confusion I picked up the grocer's hat instead of my own, and he grinned broadly as he exchanged it. This, as I said, was the happy day of my life. I might be tempted to say, the only happy day—but that would not be true. God gives us many a blessing.

"I was not at all sure what the girl might now be thinking of me. Would she be cross with me, or perhaps more favorably inclined? To pay another visit was a hard decision. But she was gentle. She sat doing some work or other, humbly and quietly, not irate as usual. She motioned with her head to a stool nearby, inviting me to sit down and help her. So we both sat there, working. The old man made as if to leave the room.

" 'Why don't you stay, Father?' she said. 'The business you have in mind is already settled.'

"He stamped his foot on the floor hard and stayed. Walking up and down he talked of this and that, and I was too shy to join in the conversation. Suddenly the girl gave a little cry. She'd scratched her finger working, and although she was not usually so sensitive, she now waved her hand up and down. I wanted to see what was the matter, but she indicated I was to go on with what I was doing.

" 'Nothing but a lot of nonsense!' the old man grumbled and, stepping right up to the girl, he said to her in a loud voice: 'The business I have in mind is by no means settled!' Then he stumped out of the room.

"I now wanted to start making excuses for yesterday's incident. But she interrupted me and said: 'Never mind about that. Let's talk of more serious things.'

"She raised her head, looked me up and down, and continued in an even voice: 'I hardly know any more how our acquaintance started, but you have been coming more and more often for some time, and we've got used to you. There's no gainsaying that you are a decent lad, but you are weak, you're always chasing after shadows, and you'd hardly be capable of looking after your own affairs.

So your friends and acquaintances are in duty bound to take a hand, to prevent you coming to harm. You sit about half the day long in the shop here, and count and weigh, measure and bargain; but there's no future in that. What do you plan to do for a living?'

"I mentioned my father's inheritance. 'I daresay it's quite a lot,' she said. I named the figure.

" 'It's a lot and yet it's not much,' she said. 'It's a lot to start something with, but not much just to spend in good living. I know my father made you a proposition, but I advised you against it. First of all he has lost money himself on this kind of thing in the past, and then,' she continued in a lower voice, 'he's so used to making his profit in dealing with strangers that he might do the same with friends. You need someone with you whose motives are honest.' I pointed to herself.

" 'I'm honest all right,' she said, and put her hand on her breast. At the same time her eyes, which usually tended toward gray, shone blue, sky-blue.

" 'But I have my own peculiar ways. Our shop here is not very profitable, and my father is playing with the idea of opening a taproom. There'd be no room for me there. The only thing left for me would be sewing, for I don't want to go into service.' She looked like a queen when she said that. 'I've been made a proposal, you know,' she continued, pulling a letter from her apron and throwing it half reluctantly on the counter, 'but it would mean I'd have to go away from here.'

" 'Far away?' I asked.

" 'Why? Why should you mind?'

"I explained that I would wish to move to the same place.

" 'You're a child,' she said. 'That wouldn't do at all and there's much more to it than that. But if you trust me and like being near me, why don't you buy the milliner's shop which is for sale next door? I know the trade and you could count on a reasonable return on your money. What's more, you yourself could find a regular occupation in looking after the accounts and all the paperwork. What else might ultimately develop, we needn't talk about now—but you would have to change. I hate effeminate men.'

"I had jumped up and reached for my hat.

" 'What's the matter?' she cried. 'Where are you going?'

" 'To cancel everything,' I said breathlessly.

" 'Cancel what?'

"I told her of my plans for setting up a copying and information agency.

" 'That isn't going to lead anywhere,' she observed. 'Information is something everybody can get for himself, and there's no one who hasn't learnt to write at school.'

"I mentioned that music was to be copied, too, which certainly was not everybody's business.

" 'Are you back on that nonsense again?' she snapped. 'Leave the music alone and stick to necessities. In any case, you wouldn't be able to manage a business yourself.'

"I explained that I had found a partner.

" 'A partner?' she exclaimed, 'I bet he's out to cheat you. You haven't paid out any money yet, have you?'

"I trembled, without knowing why.

" 'Have you paid out any money?' she insisted.

"I confessed I had advanced three thousand florins for initial installations.

" 'Three thousand florins!' she cried, "So much money!'

" 'The rest,' I continued, 'is deposited with the court and safe in any case.'

" 'Even more, then?' she shrieked.

"I told her the amount of the deposit.

" 'And did you take it yourself to the court?'

"My partner had done it, I explained.

" 'You do have a receipt for it, at least?'

"I had no receipt.

" 'And who is this fine partner of yours?' she inquired.

"With some assurance, I named my father's secretary.

" 'Heavens above!' she cried, jumping up and wringing her hands. 'Father! Father!'

"The old man came in.

" 'What is it you read in the paper today?'

" 'About the secretary?' he asked.

" 'Yes, yes!'

" 'Well, he absconded, leaving a pile of debts behind and a lot of people defrauded. They're after him with a warrant.'

" 'Father,' she cried, 'he's swindled this fellow too. He trusted him with his money. He's ruined.'

" 'What an idiot!' he yelled. 'Didn't I always say so? But she always had an excuse. She'd laugh at him, but after all he was a decent fellow. But now it's my turn. I'll show you who's master in this house. You, Barbara, off with you into the back room. And you, mister, get out and keep away in the future. We don't hand out alms here.'

" 'Father," the girl said, 'don't be too hard on him. He's unhappy enough as it is.'

" 'All the more reason why I don't want to be

unhappy as well,' the old man shouted. Pointing to the letter which Barbara had thrown on the counter, he continued: 'That, sir, that's a man! He's nobody's fool and he's got plenty of money. He doesn't cheat anyone, but he doesn't let anyone cheat him, either, and that's the better part of honesty.'

"I stuttered that the loss of the deposit wasn't certain as yet.

" 'Of course, of course, he'll have missed his best chance, our secretary!' he mocked. 'He's a scoundrel, but sharp as a needle! Run away now, perhaps you can still catch him!'

"At that he put his hand on my shoulder and pushed me toward the door. I slipped aside and turned toward the girl. She stood there, leaning against the counter, her eyes cast to the ground and her breast heaving violently up and down. I wanted to approach her, but she stamped her foot angrily on the ground, and when I held out my hand to her she raised her own hand briefly, as if she wanted to hit me again. So I left, and the old man closed the door behind me.

"I staggered through the streets, out by the gate, into the fields. Sometimes I was plunged into despair, sometimes I was hopeful. I remembered having accompanied the secretary to the commercial court to deposit the surety; I had waited in the entrance, and he had gone upstairs by himself. When he returned, he said everything was in order, and the receipt would be sent to my home. It is true that it had not arrived yet, but it might still come. At the break of day I returned to the city. My first call was at the secretary's home. But the people there laughed and asked whether I had not read the papers. The commercial court was only a few hundred yards farther on. I asked for a check in the books, but neither his name nor mine occurred in them. There was no trace of any money having been paid in. My misfortune was confirmed. Indeed, things very nearly turned out worse still, for since I was his business partner by contract, some of his creditors wanted to seek redress from me. But the courts prevented this, praise and thanks be to them! Not that it would have made any difference, anyway!

"With all these troubles, I must confess, I gave little thought to the grocer and his daughter. When things finally settled down a bit and I began to consider what to do next, the memory of the last evening with them came back with full force. The father was a selfish old man, and I could understand him well enough; but the girl? Sometimes I imagined that if only I had held on to my own and had been able to offer her a secure livelihood, she might have—. But no, she probably did not care for me." He lifted his hands and let them drop, and looked down his whole shabby person. "And she always disliked my way of being so civil to everyone.

"Thus I spent whole days, musing and turning things over in my mind. One evening at dusk, it was just the time I used to spend in the shop, I sat down and imagined myself at the familiar spot. I heard them talk, they chided me, indeed it seemed they were laughing at me. Suddenly there was a rustle at the door, it opened, and a woman came in. It was Barbara. I sat glued to my chair, as if seeing a ghost. She was pale and carried a bundle under her arm. She walked right into the middle of the room; there she stopped, looked all round at the bare walls and then down at the miserable furnishings, and sighed deeply. Then she went over to the cupboard, which stood at the side against the wall, and unwrapped her bundle which contained a few shirts and neckcloths, for she had lately looked after my washing. She opened the drawer, wrung her hands when she saw its scant contents, but then immediately started to tidy them up and to put the clean things

in their place. Then she stepped back a few paces from the cupboard, looked at me and pointed to the open drawer, and said: 'Five shirts and three neckcloths. That's what I had, that's what I bring back.' She slowly closed the drawer, supported herself with her hand against the cupboard, and began to sob. It almost seemed as if she were feeling ill, for she sat down on a chair next to the cupboard, buried her face in her kerchief, and I could hear from her gasps that she was still sobbing. I approached her quietly and took her hand, which she yielded willingly. But when, trying to make her look at me, I took her limp arm by the elbow, she quickly rose, withdrew her hand and said in a composed voice: 'What's the good of all that? Things are as they are. It's your own fault; you've made us all unhappy, us and yourself, though yourself most. You don't really deserve pity,' and she spoke more and more violently, 'being so weak that you can't keep your own affairs in order, and so credulous that you trust anybody, whether he's a rogue or an honest man. And yet I am sorry for you. I've come to say goodbye. Ah yes, you may well be startled. It's all your own doing. I've got to go out among the common people now, what I've struggled against for so long. But there's no help for it. We've already shaken hands, and so good-bye—forever.'

"I saw that her tears were welling up again, but she shook her head in vexation and went. My limbs felt as heavy as lead. When she had reached the door, she turned back once more and said: 'Your linen is in order now. See that none of it disappears. You'll be having a hard time.' She raised her hand, made the sign of the cross in the air, and cried: 'God be with you, Jacob!—For ever and ever, Amen,' she added, more softly, and went.

"At last I regained the use of my legs. I ran after her and from the top of the stairs called out: 'Barbara!' I heard her stop on the stairs. But as I descended the first step, she called from down below: 'Stay where you are!' and she walked right down and out of the front door.

"Since then I've lived through many a hard day, but none so hard as that. Even the day after was less hard. In spite of everything, I wasn't quite sure what my chances were now, and so I hung about near the grocer's shop next morning in the hope of learning some more. There was no sign of anybody. Finally I looked into the shop from the side and saw a strange woman weighing out the goods and handing out change. I ventured inside and asked whether she had bought the shop.

" 'Not yet,' she replied.

"And where were the owners?

" 'They left this morning for Langenlebarn.'

" 'The daughter, too?' I stuttered.

" 'Why of course,' she said, 'she's getting married there.'

"It may be that the woman now told me everything that I later learnt from others. The butcher from that village, the same I had met when I first called at the shop, had long made marriage proposals to the girl. She had always evaded them until the last few days, when, bullied by her father and despairing of all else, she had finally given in. This very morning father and daughter had journeyed thither, and while we were talking, Barbara was already the butcher's wife.

"The woman may have told me all this, as I said, but I didn't listen. I stood there motionless, until finally some customers came in and pushed me aside, and the woman asked me sharply whether there was anything else I wanted. I left.

"You'll believe me, dear sir," he continued, "when I say that I now considered myself the unhappiest of men. Or at any rate I did at first. But once I'd stepped out of the shop and looked back at the little windows from which Barbara had no doubt often peered out, a feeling of great peace came over me. She was free of all worry now, mistress of her own house; free of the lot that would have been hers if she had tied herself to one like me, without hearth and home; she would be spared misery and grief. All this comforted my soul like a healing balm, and I blessed her and all her ways.

"My own fortunes went on declining, and eventually I decided to try and make a living with music. As long as the remainder of my money lasted, I practiced and studied the works of the great masters, especially of the old ones, and copied them out. Once my last penny had gone, I set about putting my skill to advantage. I began with private parties, my first opportunity being an invitation on the part of my landlady. When the compositions I played failed to find favor on these occasions, I went into the courtyards of blocks of apartments, in the hope that among so many residents there would be some at least who might appreciate something serious. Eventually I played in the public thoroughfares, where at any rate I had the satisfaction that a few people stopped, listened to me, asked questions and did not walk away unmoved. I was not ashamed when they put down money for me. First of all, this was precisely my purpose, and secondly I was well aware that famous virtuosi, for whom, of course, I could not pretend to be a match, also accepted pay for their performances, and a lot of pay at times. And this is how I've made my living to this day, a scant living but an honest one.

"After many years, fortune was to smile on me once more. Barbara came back. Her husband had made some money and acquired a butcher's shop in one of the suburbs. She has two children, of whom the elder is called Jacob, like me. My professional occupations and my memories of old times prevented me from pressing myself upon her, but eventually I was called to their home, and they asked me to give violin lessons to their boy. Admittedly he hasn't much talent, and in any case he can play only on Sundays, because his father employs him in the shop during the week, but Barbara's song, which I taught him, he manages to play quite well already. Sometimes, when we are busy practicing together, his mother joins in and sings with us. She has changed a lot in all these years, she is fat now and has little thought of music, but nevertheless it sounds as pretty as ever."

With these words the old man picked up his violin again and began playing the song, and

played on and on without taking any further notice of me. At last I got bored, put down a few silver coins on the table and went away, while the old man still fiddled with zest.

Soon afterward I set out on a journey and did not return until the onset of winter. New impressions crowded out the old ones, and my old fiddler was all but forgotten. It was not until the big thaw of the following spring, and the disastrous floods which occurred in the low-lying suburbs, that I thought of him again. The neighborhood of Gärtnergasse had become a lake. The old man's life was probably not in danger, seeing that he lived high up just under the roof, and death had picked his all too numerous victims from among the ground-floor dwellers. But he would be cut off from all help and might be in great need. While the inundation lasted, nothing could be done, and the authorities were doing their best to get food and assistance to the marooned people. As soon as the waters subsided and it became possible to walk again in the streets, I decided that I would in person take my contribution to the huge relief fund, which was then being collected, to the sufferer about whom I was most concerned.

Leopoldstadt looked appalling. The streets

were full of shattered boats and household goods; in many houses the ground floor was still under water, on which people's possessions were floating about. Once, when I stepped aside from the throng, through a gate that stood ajar, I found myself in a courtyard entry where a row of corpses had been laid out—evidently for the official inspection; here and there in the rooms the drowned could still be seen standing and clutching at the window bars—there simply was not time enough nor were there officials enough to certify so many deaths.

I went on walking. On every side weeping and bells tolling, mothers searching and lost children wandering about. At last I reached Gärtnergasse. Here too the black-garbed undertaker's men were lined up for a funeral, though it seemed they were not anywhere near the house I was seeking. However, when I came nearer, I saw that there was some connection, in the shape of preparations and people coming and going, between the funeral procession and the gardener's house. At the door of the house stood a hearty-looking man, elderly, but still vigorous. In his knee-length boots, yellow leather breeches and long frock coat, he looked like a country butcher. He was giving orders and in between talking casually with the bystanders. I went past him, and inside the gardener's old wife came forward, recognized me at once, and greeted me through her tears.

"You've come to do us the honor?" she said. "Our poor old man," she went on, "he's playing his fiddle now among the angels, who can't be much more angelic than he was on earth. The good old soul was sitting safely up there in his room. But when the water came and he heard the children crying, he ran down and rescued them and lugged and carried and dragged them to safety, till he was puffing and blowing like a blacksmith's bellows. And then—you can't think of everything, can you?—when at last we discovered that my husband had left his account books and a few florins of paper money in the wall cupboard, the old man took an axe, plunged into the water which came up to his chest, broke open the cupboard and faithfully brought everything back. I expect he caught a chill. And then at first we couldn't get any help, and he began to be delirious, and got worse and worse, though we did all we could for him, and it was harder for us than for him. He just lay there and played away, with the voice of course, and beat time and gave lessons. When the water had gone down a little and we could fetch the surgeon and priest, he suddenly sat up in bed, turned his head to one side as though he heard something very beautiful far away, smiled, lay back again, and died. Do go up, he often spoke about you. The lady is upstairs, too. We wanted to pay for his funeral, but the butcher's lady wouldn't let us."

She urged me up the steep stairs to the room in the roof. It was open, and bare of everything except the coffin in the center, already closed and only waiting for the bearers. At the head sat a stoutish woman, getting on in years, dressed in a bright, printed cotton skirt, but with a black neckerchief and a black ribbon on her bonnet. It was hard to believe that she could ever have been pretty. Before her stood two quite big children, a boy and a girl, whom she was evidently instructing on how to behave at the funeral. Just as I went in she pushed the boy's arm away from the coffin on which he was gawkily leaning, and then carefully smoothed out the corner of the pall. The gardener's wife introduced me, but just then the trombones down below began to sound, and the butcher called up from the road: "Barbara! It's time!" The bearers appeared, and I drew back to make room. The coffin was lifted up, taken downstairs and the procession started to move off. In front were schoolchildren with cross and banner, then the priest and sacristan. Immediately behind the coffin went the butcher's children, and their parents. The husband was continually moving his lips as though in prayer, but at the same time looking to right and left. His wife studied her prayer book, though the two children gave her plenty to do; she kept pushing them forward and then holding them back, and altogether seemed to set much store by a proper and orderly procession. But she always turned back to her book. At last we reached the cemetery. The grave was open. The children threw in the first handful of earth. Their father then did likewise, still standing, while his wife knelt and held her prayer book close to her eyes. The gravediggers finished their business and the procession, which had begun to break up, turned back. At the gates there was a bit of an argument; the butcher's wife evidently considered the charges too high. Then the mourners separated and went away. And that was the old fiddler's burial.

A few days later–it was a Sunday–I went, at the prompting of my psychological curiosity, to the butcher's house. My pretext was that I would like to have the old man's violin as a memento of him. I found the family assembled and showing no sign of any lasting impression. And yet the

violin was hanging on the wall, beside the mirror, in symmetry with a crucifix on the other side. When I explained my mission and offered a fairly high price, the husband seemed not disinclined to do a profitable bit of business. But his wife jumped up from her chair and said: "Nothing of the sort! The fiddle belongs to our Jacob, and a few florins more or less won't make any different to us." Whereupon she took the violin down from the wall, blew the dust off it, looked at it from all sides and placed it in a drawer which she vigorously closed and locked, as though she were afraid of robbery. As she did so, her face was turned away from me, so that I could not see her expression. Just then the maid came in with the soup. The butcher, indifferent to the presence of a visitor, boomed out his grace before meat, in which the shrill voices of the children joined, and I wished them a pleasant meal and went out. My last glimpse was of the woman. She had turned round, and I saw that tears were streaming down her cheeks.